Seven Wild Pigs

Seven Wild Pigs

Eleven Picture Book Fantasies

Helme Heine

Translated from the German

Margaret K. McElderry Books

NEW YORK

Published originally under the title: Sieben Wilde Schweine by Gertraud Middelhauve Verlag, Köln
© Copyright 1986 by Gertraud Middelhauve Verlag GmbH & Co. KG, Köln
English translation copyright © 1988 by Margaret K. McElderry Books, a division of Macmillan Publishing Company

Margaret K. McElderry Books
Macmillan Publishing Company
866 Third Avenue
New York, NY 10022

First American Edition

Printed in Germany

10 9 8 7 6 5 4 3 2 1

Library of Congress Cataloging-in-Publication Data

Heine, Helme.
Seven wild pigs.

Translation of: Sieben wilde Schweine.
Summary: A collection of stories, many in rhyme, about
such things as a hungry crocodile, a foolish artist, the
value of drinking apple juice, and how it feels to be a
bottle.
1. Children's stories, German—Translations into
English. 2. Children's stories, English—Translations
from German. [1. Stories in rhyme. 2. Short stories]
I. Title.
PZ8.3.H41343Se 1988   [E]   87-3448
ISBN 0-689-50439-X

Good Appetite!

This crocodile
Eats quite a pile!

Snaring a heron by its legs,
He ate it up, plus twenty eggs;

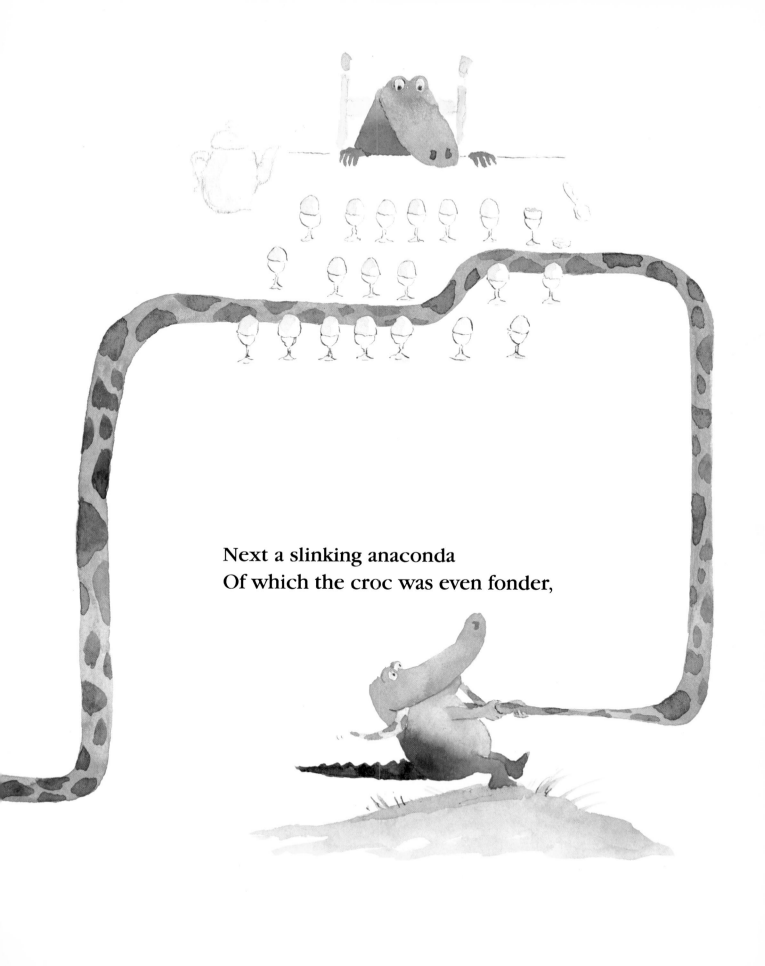

Next a slinking anaconda
Of which the croc was even fonder,

An elephant, its tusks and all,

And something else I don't recall.

That did not fill him up, so then

He gobbled down an ostrich hen,

A hippo and an aged priest,
A very tough and bony feast.

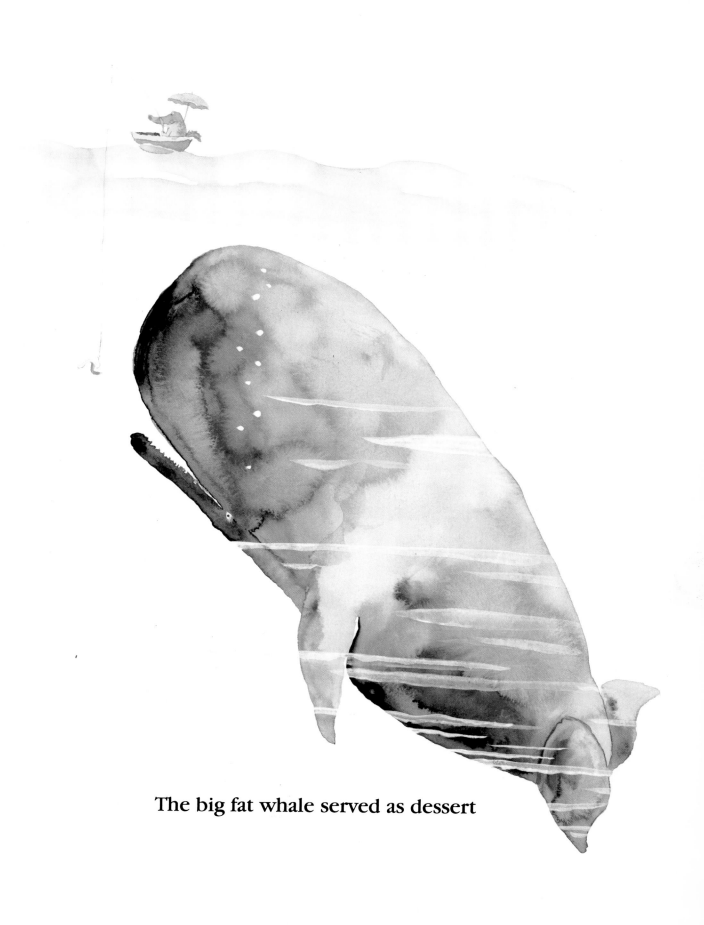

The big fat whale served as dessert

Which turned him slowly less alert.

He burped and then was heard to say,
"I don't need much more food today."

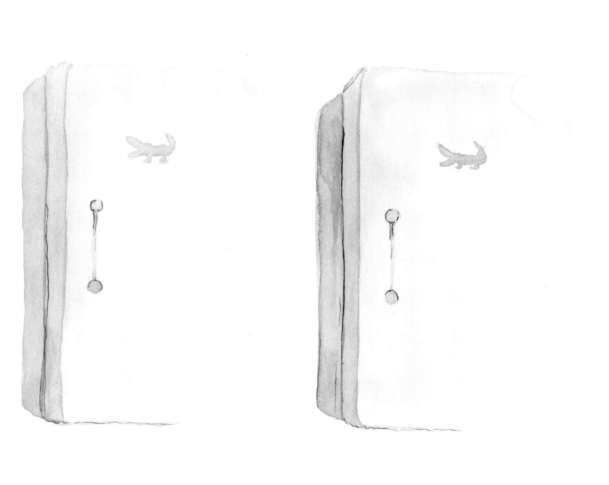

The Great and the Small

"My son," the woodworm said at home,
"Enjoy your life, enjoy this throne!"

The mighty king—I should mention—
Did not pay them much attention—

Until one day he lost his throne, and
The woodworm moved to another home.

The moral that this tale evokes:
"Do not ignore the little folks!"

Seven Wild Pigs

An artist painted the forest home
Of seven wild pigs, who liked to roam.

Impudently they scampered there,
Scattering colors everywhere.

Though they themselves felt happy and smart,
It was clear they had no feeling for art.

The poor painter
had had enough.
"Buzz off, you pigs,
or I'll get tough!"

They trotted off behind the trees,
Grunting and snorting, to torment and tease.

The artist then turned angry and mean
And leaped into the forest scene.
With five quick strokes, the clever fellow
Painted a hut with a roof of yellow.

Whoosh!—the front door opened fast.
Out jumped a dog and raced on past.
Next came a hunter with his gun
To get those wild pigs every one.

A horn blows,
A rifle goes—
One, two, three, four, five, six, seven—
All good piggies went to heaven!

For supper, roast pork at half past nine,
Cranberry sauce and fine white wine.
The painter was not the least suspicious.
He thought it all tasted quite delicious.

But soon he realized what they had done.
Why, they had eaten the smallest one!
He thanked his hosts and said good-bye.
Had he dreamed it all, he thought with a sigh.

But no—bullet holes were everywhere!
It gave the artist quite a scare!
He shivered, he shook, he got the creeps,
His beautiful painting was ruined for keeps.

"Never again," the artist swore,
"I'll never paint wild pigs anymore!"

Apple juice, the latest hit,
Quenches thirst and keeps you fit.

The Latest Hit

Once the apple juice is drunk
There is nothing left but junk.

Mail in a Bottle

Imagine you're a bottle.
You stand around, waiting to be bought.
Then the door opens.

A pirate enters the store and picks you out.
There's some luck in that, of course—
not many bottles are bought by pirates.

The pirate takes you on board,
hoists the anchor and sails away.
You're caught in a storm, the mainmast breaks,
the ship crashes on a rock and goes under.

You and the pirate escape to a small,
deserted island.
The pirate drinks you empty,
But not because he's in despair.
He needs you to send
some mail in a bottle.

He writes a few lines to his mother,
sticks the letter inside you,
and throws you back in the sea.
You swim home to his mother by the shortest route.
She has been waiting anxiously for mail from her son.

She reads the letter
and sets off
to rescue her son
from the lonely island.

In gratitude, the pirate builds
a small sailing ship

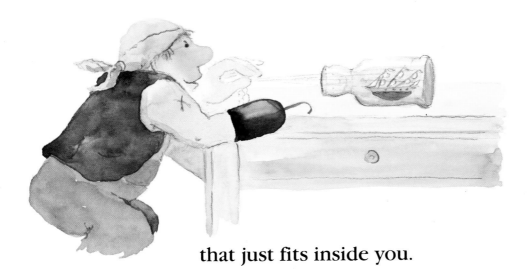

that just fits inside you.

He gives it to his mother for her birthday.

That makes her very happy.

Yes, life can be exciting!
Especially if you're a bottle or a pirate
or the mother of a pirate.

The Champion

An ostrich who won every race
Wanted to make a change of pace.
He set his sights a little higher
And aspired to be a champion flyer.
Next morning, at five past ten,
The ostrich climbed a rock, and then
He stretched his neck and spread his wings,
Poised to take off for greater things.
This should have been his finest hour.
Alas, he lacked the flying power.
He fell to earth and broke his neck.
He left this world a total wreck.
All in deepest mourning dressed,
They laid the champion to rest.
No eye was dry, no word was said.
Instead, his tombstone clearly read:
"Here all may see my body lie,
But not my soul, for that can fly!"

The Diary of

Johnny Mouse

New Year's brought an avalanche of snow.
I love sledding as much as bicycle riding—
especially downhill!

I had to talk Charlie Rooster and fat Percy
into making snowmen. They didn't want to at first.
But now they're very proud of them.
I hope no one swipes the carrot.

We decorated the barn together and
celebrated Mardi Gras for a whole week.
It was terrific. I'm already looking forward
to next year.

Fat Percy saw the Easter Bunny with his very
own eyes. He was riding on a chicken.
(Charlie says that's impossible!)

Charlie has changed his mind. He sat right
on a chocolate egg. It took him a long time to
wipe the smear out of his feathers!

We hardly have had any time to play lately.
There's so much to do. Today the field had
to be tilled. Fat Percy plowed, I sowed the seeds,
and Charlie took care of the pests.

After milking, we played cowboys and Indians.
Even Aunt Millie had a good time.
Charlie was the only one who grumbled.
He didn't like being the Indian all the time.

I flew ten feet today. Charlie did, too.
It's just like riding a bicycle without touching
the ground. I want to be a pilot.

Fat Percy was jealous, because he can't fly.
Only after I convinced him of my friendship
was he happy again.

Charlie has been sick. Now he's well again,
and he went swimming with us.
We had to talk him into coming,
because he is so ashamed without his feathers.
Percy said he shouldn't make such a fuss. After all,
he goes around without anything on all the time.

Lame Anna Cruikshank fell asleep on her nest
and never woke up again. She looked so peaceful.
I wonder where she is now.

I visited the grave by the great Stone Egg
and took some flowers for Anna Cruikshank.
Gray Lilly sits on her nest now.

We saved the life of a young lady rabbit.
She's called Knuff-Knuff and is as pretty as a picture.
Too bad she's not a mouse.
In gratitude she presented us with three carrots.
Later we found out they came from our own garden!

I hate chopping wood! Every time Percy—the big jerk—
hacks a piece of my whiskers off and then laughs at me.
That's only because he doesn't have whiskers.

Fog, fog, fog everywhere. Riding your bike is no fun
if you can't see where you're going.
Tomorrow we're putting it up in the attic.
Winter is waiting at the barn door.

I still can't believe my good luck.
I found Santa Claus's left mitten.
Maybe he dropped it on purpose,
because he must have known
how much I wanted a sleeping bag.
It's great to have friends and a warm bed.

Brief Happiness

Rhino loves train.
Train leaves for Maine.
Rhino in pain.

The Spider

Hi, folks!
You know girls
are silly.
They see ghosts
everywhere.

At night,
around sundown,
they mistake
every pumpkin
in the garden
for a giant.

And if they have to get
something out of
the cellar,
they get goose bumps
as big as nickels.

If a black cat crosses
their path in the dark,
they get so scared
they can't sleep
for three nights.

Fiddle-faddle!
Just look at that!
Running away
from a spider!
What a nut!

Benjamin

Or a Hero's Deed

Benjamin had had it.

All his life he had cowered in fear before Lou Cat.
He had shivered and quivered and had hidden from him.
But now he was going to show him.

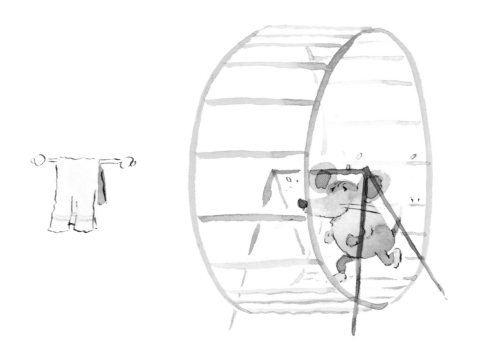

He started jogging every morning,
long before sunrise, on the hamster's wheel.
He lifted barbells, and every day he put on weight.

He boxed the tennis ball for ten rounds
and chopped macaroni in half
with his bare hand to harden himself.

He could do nine and a half push-ups,
and he chinned himself fourteen times
and swam the full length of the aquarium
in record time, all at the risk of his life.

He hung from the clothesline by his tail
for sixty seconds,
till the blood pounded in his temples.
He toughened himself on the hedgehog.

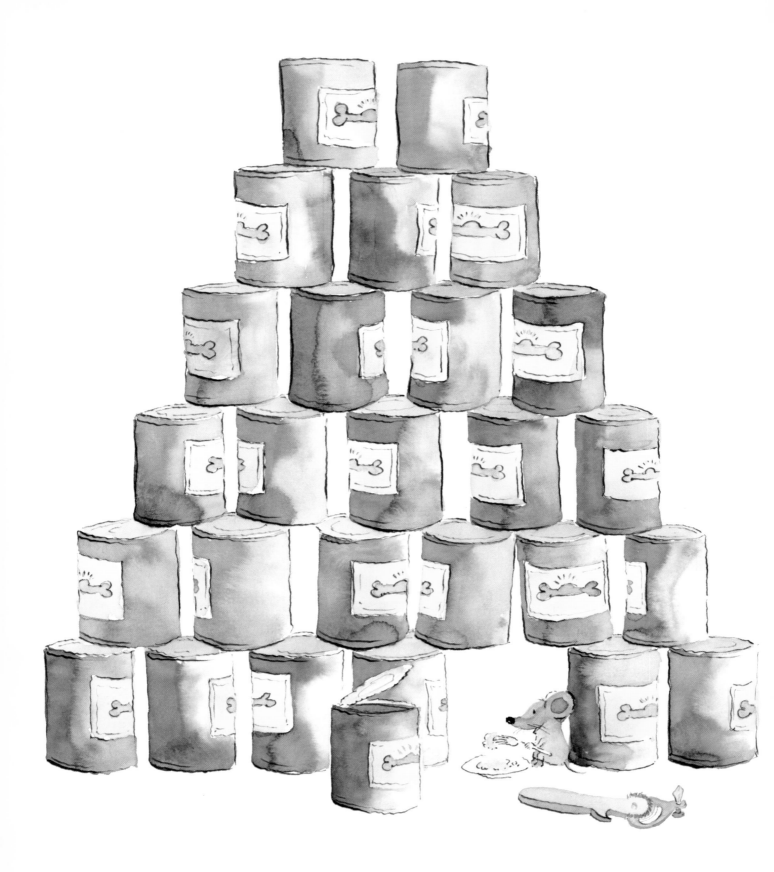

Every day he devoured a big can of special body-building food.
Finally he felt strong enough to confront his deadly enemy.

He crept up to Lou Cat from behind,
every tendon taut, every muscle poised at its peak.
He showed him unmistakably what he thought of him.

Then, with a flying leap, he bounded to safety.

The Crazy Farm

The goose is featherless and fat.

The mouse attacks the cat.

The hen could use five socks.   The bee collects the rocks.

The cow produces beer.

The goat plays Gershwin here.

The pig sleeps late—it's on strike.

The ducks enjoy the motorbike.

The farmer lays an egg each day. It's just like Christmas Eve in May.

Six days of the week they are lazy,
and those who believe it are crazy.